Story Town is a series of illustrated stories which are posted online every couple of hours to keep you company throughout your day.

At times, there is interaction from readers who are experiencing it live. They are asked to make decisions about the story, or complete tasks to achieve a certain outcome.

The choices and tasks for "To Lumber Home" are collected near the end of this book.

To read a Story Town as it runs,
go to *www.story-town.com*
New stories begin on the first Monday of the month.

For anyone who has ever had to leave.

For anyone who needs to.

TO LUMBER HOME

By Jason Albin Thomas

It is often the case that people born in the same family act very differently, even though they were raised the same way. You might have a very sweet disposition, while your brother or sister is very spiteful and bitter all the time.

Or perhaps *you* are the awful one.

But this is not a story about how dreadful you are, or your delightful sibling. That would be a boring story that you (and the people who have to deal with you) already know quite well.

Bears are much like people when it comes to how different their temperaments can be. Some bear cubs just start life out angry, while some are lazy. Many bears are interested in sweet things like honey, while some like sour flavors. Some like to play, while others like hunting best.

This is a story about a bear. It is about other things as well, but it begins with a bear.

It is not about *this* bear, however. This bear would eventually be known as "Kaskov," who liked to drink out of bottles he had found.

I would like very much to tell you that he eventually grew out of this habit, but he never did.

This story is about a bear who would one day be named Pilot. He was fascinated by people, even when he was just a little cub.

This was strange behavior for a bear, but he couldn't help but be interested in people. He loved watching them work in the woods, gathering trees to be cut into lumber. They were always busy moving wood from one place to the next. The little bear felt that he wouldn't mind working hard if it meant he could be friends with the men at the lumber mill.

The bear often wondered what all that wood was for, and why the men worked so hard to gather it.

"All that wood is probably used to make people things," he thought to himself.

He was too little, as a cub, but he promised himself that once he was older, he would have the courage to go down to the lumber mill and see if they would let him work with the men there.

He knew he could be very helpful if they would only let him try.

One day, when he was old enough, that is just what he did.

Pilot was very nervous about approaching the men at the lumber mill. He had always been taught to be wary of people, and that they might be scared of a bear.

"Fear makes humans dangerous," his mother had taught him. "They often hurt what they are afraid of."

The men at the lumber mill did not know what to think of the bear at first. They had always been taught to be afraid of bears, but this one seemed intent on helping.

They considered it for a while, and everyone turned to Heck Bodkins to see what he would say. Heck was a bully, and everyone was a little afraid of him, so no one liked to give their opinion until Heck had given his. Everyone usually agreed with him to avoid trouble.

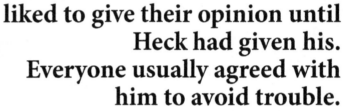

"Having a bear around could be handy," Heck whispered to the other men. "Bears are too stupid to know what money is. We wouldn't have to pay him."

"And another thing," Heck went on. "Any work this bear does, is work we don't have to do."

Everyone agreed that it sounded like a good idea to them.

They tried teaching the bear to mark which trees should be cut down, but he was unable to tell the difference between which trees were ready and which were not.

They hoped the bear might learn to use the big saw to cut the logs down into planks, but the noise was so loud that it scared him. He covered his head and whimpered until they turned it off again.

The bear tried to make himself useful by preparing a special breakfast for everyone. "If they like it, they will keep me around. The men will want more breakfasts like these, and they will love having me around."

"I will cover these fish with honey, just to be extra sure the nice men enjoy them," the bear thought.

A dead fish with honey smeared all over it is a rare and beloved delicacy to a bear.

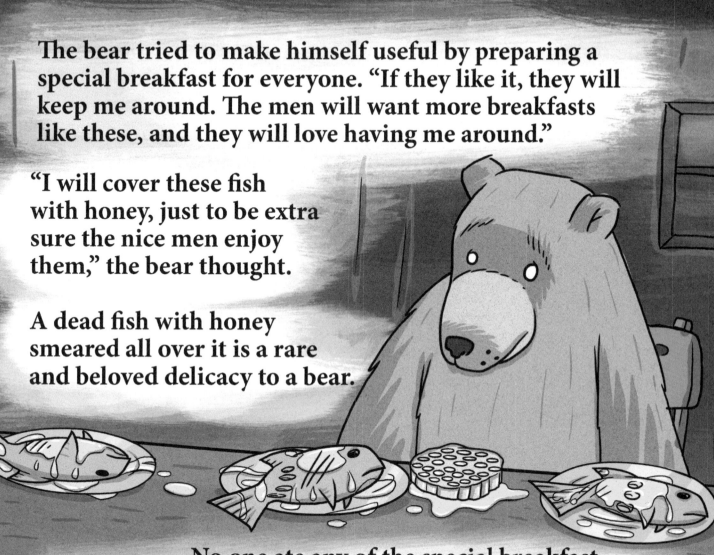

No one ate any of the special breakfast. In fact, the men laughed and called it "bearly edible". Usually the bear would have just eaten all of the breakfasts himself, but he was too despondent to eat.

The men came to learn one thing that the bear could do reliably: place the wood into tidy, carefully made piles. He was strong and would do this all day without complaint. They would give lumber to the bear, point to where they wanted it to go, say "pile it," and he would.

The men said "pile it" to the bear so often in fact, that they just started calling him that.

Pilot was pleased to have been given a people-name.

Heck Bodkins made fun of the bear, and he encouraged the other workers to, as well. Pilot was different, and this made everyone uneasy.

Pilot suspected that the teasing weakened him in their eyes, and made them feel less afraid. He considered that perhaps it was a good thing for them to be less afraid.

Knowing this did not keep his feelings from being hurt, however.

You may have heard the term "Mean as heck." It is a very old saying, but Heck Bodkins was old enough and mean enough that the phrase may originally been about him.

Heck had been unhappy for so long that he no longer knew how to be any other way. He spent his time bullying, gossiping, causing misery, and spreading hate wherever he went. It was as if Heck wanted to make everyone as unhappy and hateful as he was, so he could feel normal.

I do not know if he truly thought this out or not. He was probably just a mean person. Some people are just mean.

For a long, long while, Pilot hoped to be accepted by the men at the lumber mill.

He would sleep outside the bunk house and listen to the men as they played cards, laughed, and had a fine time. He wondered if they were laughing about him.

Pilot knew they did not want him around because he was a bear, but he felt if he was patient and worked extra hard he would eventually be invited to play the cards, listen to the jokes, and make friends.

But he never was.

One day when it was raining, Heck stood alongside the log truck. He had just come back from town, and was talking to some of the men.

He was bragging about how he had hit so many animals with the truck along the way.

Heck boasted that even if an animal saw him coming, he was lightning quick and could swerve to hit them every time.

He laughed hard about the noises they made when they hit the front of the truck and died.

When everyone had gone, Pilot pulled a dead creature from the front of the truck. It was still and cold. It looked like a raccoon, but he wasn't sure.

He wondered if it had felt any hurt before it had died.

He wondered if it had a family, and if they would be worried.

It wouldn't come back home tonight.

It would never come back home again, ever.

Pilot no longer wanted to be accepted by the men at the lumber mill. He didn't want to be there at all anymore.

Pilot left.

He did not know where he would go.

But he felt anywhere would be better than where he had been.

For months, Pilot walked away from the lumber mill. As Pilot went, the woods became unfamiliar.

He did not know where the river was in these woods, so finding food had become difficult.

It takes courage to leave a place, even if it is awful. Pilot didn't realize he was being brave by leaving, but he was. It takes a lot of courage to make a change.

Now, we know Pilot was being brave, but all Pilot knew was his stomach hurting from hunger and that he was all alone.

It can take time, but eventually you may find your place if you look hard enough.

The people of Story Town might not be accepting of a bear, and Pilot knew this. He realized that many bears were violent. Many bears would maul a person to death if they felt threatened, were having a bad day, were hungry, or wanted to fill the time with an exciting activity.

Pilot was sweet and gentle, and would never maul a person, but they wouldn't know that.

"Perhaps they will be more comfortable with a man in a bear *costume* than an actual bear," he thought to himself.

Pilot found some discarded paint in the woods and painted stitches and buttons on himself. He thought they looked very convincing, and was quite pleased with their realism.

Pilot walked into town to look for work.

Some cats love being inside all the time, because that is what they are used to, but before Zipper had come to live with the Froogs, he could come and go as he pleased. He had gotten used to having outside adventures by the old lighthouse where he was raised.

Zipper the cat was not supposed to go outside, but he couldn't resist the call of adventure.

Whenever the door was left open a crack, he would begin inching towards it as quietly as a butterfly's wings brushing against a flower petal.

His family remembered, how when Zipper first came to them, he was very close to death.

Sally Froog (Often worries about Zipper).

Barnabus Froog (Has recurring nightmares in which Zipper is hit by a car or eaten by a tiger).

"Nickel" Froog (Frequently leaves the door open).

Buttons

It had been a while since Zipper had been able to escape and go downtown. He was looking forward to visiting Worldsworst's Diner, which was his favorite place.

The owner of the diner would often make him a plate of food whenever the diner was empty, which was usually the case.

He would have to sneak Zipper in, because having an animal in the diner would be a health code violation.

WORLDSWORST'S DINER OPENING DAY!

Wallace Worldsworst had always dreamed of opening a diner. He had fond memories of them from when he was a child. Wallace saved money for years and years, and was finally able to afford a little spot for his diner.

If my last name was "Worldsworst" I would not have named a diner after myself, but then again, it has not been my lifelong dream to own one.

Wallace did know his name would be a challenge, and took steps to ensure that anyone who ate at Worldsworst's Diner did not think it was *actually* the world's worst diner.

Little Mike was the best chef that Wallace could find. He told Wallace that he had worked on a ship, preparing meals for the crew and passengers. Wallace liked the idea of hiring a well-travelled chef from a fancy cruise ship.

Little Mike was the smallest of his eight brothers, and had always been the last to eat. As a result, he grew up obsessed with food.

Chef Mike's food was beyond reproach. His sandwiches were exquisite works of art and his soups were like kissing a moonbeam. The hash that Chef Mike created was like having a warm hug from the mom on your favorite television program. No one ever ate at Worldsworst's Diner without thinking that Little Mike's cooking was some of the best food they had ever eaten in their lives.

When Worldsworst's Diner first opened its doors, many tourists began to arrive, and it seemed that things were going very well. People from all around the world came to Story Town just to experience the "World's Worst Diner."

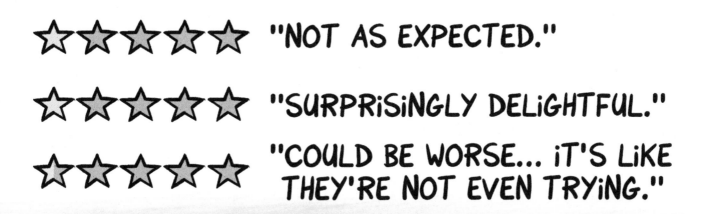

☆☆☆☆☆ "NOT AS EXPECTED."

☆☆☆☆☆ "SURPRiSiNGLY DELiGHTFUL."

★★★★★ "COULD BE WORSE... iT'S LiKE THEY'RE NOT EVEN TRYiNG."

People were curious about how bad the diner could be, and they were terribly disappointed when they found it to be neat and tidy with wonderful food.

One critic wrote, in a particulary scathing review, "The world's BEST diner is more like it!"

These days, hardly anyone ate at the diner except Zipper.

Worldsworst's would be out of business before long.

On the day Pilot came in looking for a job, Wallace had been drinking. He had been drinking the rest of the days, as well. Wallace was taking the imminent demise of his lifelong dream very hard.

The guy in the bear costume was quiet, but he seemed nice enough to Wallace. He thought he might as well try it out, and hoped that perhaps the tourists would write their reviews about the guy in a bear costume, instead of complaining about unbroken egg yolks and uncharred toast.

Pilot was never told what to do at the diner, so he just wandered into the kitchen and started preparing food. Pilot was nervous about how people would like his cooking after the men at the lumber mill had laughed at him so cruelly.

He did not know many food recipes, so he made his trout covered with honey.

Whenever Pilot got honeycomb out of logs, he was stung a lot. It hurt, but it was worth it. Pilot knew that bees were determined and easily angered. Some of the bees followed him into the diner, but that could not be avoided.

By the second day, Pilot had watched Little Mike and learned how to make all sorts of things.

Cooking seemed to be very easy to Pilot. He learned that a sandwich was food between two things, while a soup was warm water with food in it.

An omelette was egg with some pieces of food folded inside that you weren't using for anything else.

Pilot was becoming more comfortable in the kitchen, and before long he was making up his own foods to serve.

You may already know this, but a bear will often choose foods that smell the strongest over foods that smell the most delicious. Pilot was no exception.

He would spend the morning rummaging around the woods or the garbage cans to find things for his recipes. Pilot's cooking upset Little Mike terribly, and one day he left without saying a word, leaving Pilot in charge of all the dishes that were prepared at Worldsworst's Diner.

During Pilot's first week at the diner, two people became very ill and one died.

Worldsworst's Diner did not get into trouble regarding the man who died, because he never actually ate any of Pilot's cooking. He had a weak heart, and the sight of the dish had frightened him to death. The man had been clutching his fork and knife so tightly that they had to be buried with him.

As a precaution, Wallace was ordered to post a notice on the door that people with a weak constitution should avoid eating at Worldsworst's Diner.

Once the news spread that a man had died of fright after merely *looking* at a dish from the diner, the tourists started taking notice. Thrill seekers from around the globe came to try out what was surely the worst diner the world had ever known.

The diner became packed with people who longed to experience the horrors within. Crowds lined up outside as Worldsworst's Diner served Pilot's terrible cuisine as fast as he could heap it onto plates. Customers watched with delight as patrons ran outside and became ill in the street.

It had become a dangerous game, and people wanted to know if they could keep their food down, then boast to their friends about it later.

Pilot made several dishes which did not disappoint customers who were expecting remarkably terrible food.

One of his more interesting creations was called "Ladybug Picnic."

It was a biscuit served on a piece of cardboard from the trash, adorned with ladybugs and a cat tail with a worm wrapped around it.

Pilot always made sure every dish was served with a pine cone, sometimes two.

Pilot found that you could do many things with a pine cone. You could scratch with it, for one thing. Scratching always felt good.

You could probably even eat one.

Pilot felt that pretty much everyone deserved to have a pine cone, and since they were so easy to find, there was never an additional charge.

Many customers did try to eat them, and cut their mouths until they bled. Fans of the diner called it "The Kindest Cut," and cited it as a critical part of the Worldsworst's experience.

You are probably wondering how no one noticed that Pilot was a real bear, as his costume was not very convincing.

After all, when you saw Pilot on the cover of this story, you were probably not fooled by it. The answer is simply this: sometimes people do not notice things if they do not *expect* them.

It's just like the Owl of Fortune, for example.

As you may already know, the Owl of Fortune is an owl who sometimes visits and if a person notices him, he will give them the thing they need most in that moment. That is of course why he is known as the "Owl of Fortune."

However, it is very, very rare for a person to notice him because, just like a large bear working in a diner, people do not expect to see an owl in their home among the books and other things on the shelf.

The Owl of Fortune may be visiting you right now, but you are busy reading this story and have not seen him. Perhaps you should take a moment to look around and see if he is there, staring at you.

I will wait while you search for him.

Pilot was glad that everyone presumed he was a person in a bear costume. He knew he would not be welcome to live in the town if anyone realized what he was. Pilot would certainly not be allowed to cook in the diner anymore, as that would be a health code violation.

Also, people would be afraid that he might maul them.

Pilot found an old rusty dumpster behind the diner and converted it into an apartment for himself, where he sat when he wasn't working. He didn't want to push his luck, and had to be careful about how much he walked around in public.

For a long time, Pilot kept to himself and did not make friends. He did love being around people, and enjoyed cooking for them, but Pilot was quite lonely. He felt unaccepted, which of course he was.

Have you ever seen a cat staring off into space for a long time? That happens because cats are some of the world's great *noticers*. When that happens, they are thinking cat thoughts and noticing things that you do not.

Being a cat, Zipper noticed things. He could tell that Pilot was a real bear, and also that he was alone in the world.

Zipper started following Pilot everywhere. He had never seen a bear before, but he had heard about them. He had heard that bears were savage, and could eat a person up as fast as you please. Zipper had also heard that a bear's growl could turn you as white as a ghost for the rest of your days.

Zipper didn't know if those things were true, but Pilot seemed very nice. He was clearly a different sort of bear.

It is actually quite difficult to find a friend when your species has a reputation for tearing things apart and eating them if they are smaller than you, especially when *most* creatures are smaller than you.

Because of this, Pilot had never had a friend of any sort before now.

Have you ever been without any friends at all? That is how Pilot had lived his entire life.

Zipper started visiting Pilot at the diner every day that he could. He would sometimes bring him cat litter or dead bugs for recipes.

They walked together often, and each day became closer.

The bear and the cat became best friends.

Soon, they were ridiculous for one another.

We Have CORN!

44

Often, the two had to be apart. Pilot had to work at the diner and Zipper could not escape the Froogs every day.

Pilot invented a thing he called a "Friendship Box." It was made from wood, string, and glue. He painted it true blue, because that is what Pilot felt a good friendship should be.

He also decorated it with buttons. "Buttons are fancy," Pilot thought to himself. "These buttons will make the box look important."

The way the Friendship Box worked was simple. One friend could place an item in the box for another friend to find, then that friend could do the same in return.

Pilot and Zipper would leave each other candy, a little note, or something Pilot had carved out of wood.

Sometimes they would leave the box in a spot they both knew, or they would make a game of hiding it. Sometimes Pilot would take it to Worldsworst's Diner and later, Zipper would come and get it from him.

Another thing that Pilot invented, for days that Zipper could not escape the Froog home, was staring through the window.

For hours.

At this point, the Froog family did not suspect that Pilot was a real bear, but it was still quite upsetting.

Zipper and Pilot would scratch at the side of the house when they were bored and lonely for each other's company.

Over time, a hole formed through the wall that was large enough for the Friendship Box to fit through.

It was at this point that the Froogs began to suspect that Pilot was a real bear.

Barnabus Froog did not mind the widening hole in the wall as much as he worried about the little cat.

Barnabus loved Zipper dearly, and was very concerned about his befriending a bear.

Whenever they could be together, it was glorious.

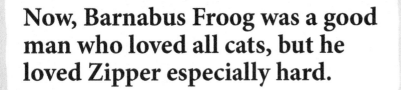

Now, Barnabus Froog was a good man who loved all cats, but he loved Zipper especially hard.

Barnabus Froog was also a worrier, and he especially worried about Zipper.

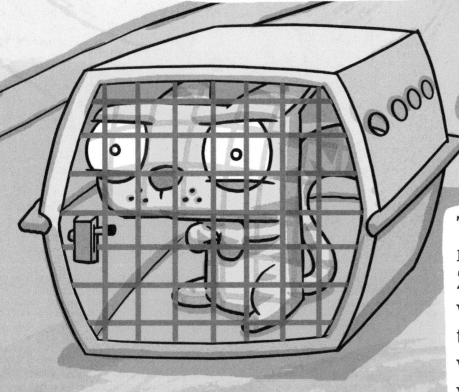

There seemed to be no way to keep Zipper from playing with the bear, except to lock him in a crate when he wasn't being watched.

Zipper hurried to Worldsworst's Diner to exchange items in the Friendship Box. Pilot would often hide it near the dumpster for him to find.

Zipper was excited, on that particular day, because it was a Tuesday, and those were the *best* days for exchanging items. On Tuesdays, they only traded things they made themselves.

Zipper sometimes put on little plays using insects he caught. When he did this, Pilot laughed until tears rolled down his cheeks.

Zipper had made a tiny magician to put in the Friendship Box. He had named him "The Amazing Beetleby" and couldn't wait to hear Pilot laugh about it.

During his break, Pilot went out to place the Friendship Box by the dumpster. He would hide it well enough to make it fun, but not so well that Zipper could not find it.

Pilot was excited about what he had made for Zipper, and wondered what he would find inside the box later on. He hoped that Zipper had dressed up another insect. The last one had been a detective named "Inspector Cricket," and it had been very funny.

Pilot wondered if he would find Inspector Cricket's assistant, or if it would be something new.

When a bear wants to, he can move very, very fast.

Pilot knew the truck. He knew who was driving it, and what that meant.

To onlookers, it seemed there would be enough time for the man in the bear costume to grab the little cat, and get him to safety.

Pilot knew that wasn't so.

There wouldn't be time for that.

The sound was heard throughout town, and a crowd of concerned people gathered to see.
Not a single word was spoken.

The great bear's arms, which had kept Zipper safe from the impact of the truck, were now still and limp.

Zipper touched the great bear across his face, hoping for a breath... hoping he would open his eyes and get up. That there was still life in the sweet and gentle bear.

JUST A DUMB OLD BEAR...

The gathered crowd did not hear Heck Bodkins' words. They were thinking about how nice the man in the bear costume had been. They wished they had gotten to know him better, and shook their heads at how tragic it was that a sweet and interesting man was now gone from them.

They also wondered how Worldsworst's Diner could possibly find anyone to cook as wonderfully, and terribly, as Pilot had.

After a time, several people tried to call Zipper, or pull the little cat away, but he would not leave his friend.

Zipper just stayed very still and stared off into space.

Cats are some of the world's great noticers.

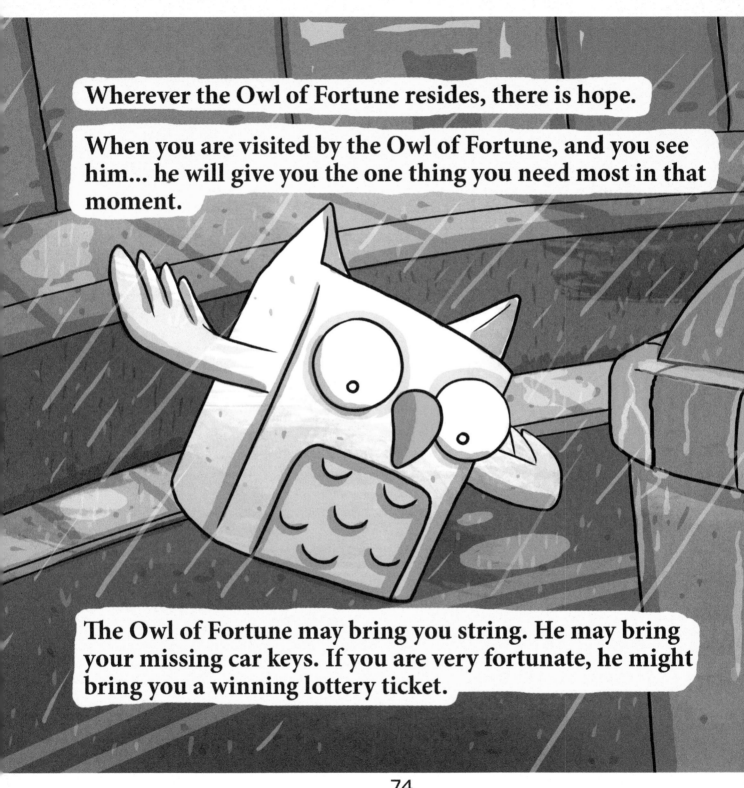

Wherever the Owl of Fortune resides, there is hope.

When you are visited by the Owl of Fortune, and you see him... he will give you the one thing you need most in that moment.

The Owl of Fortune may bring you string. He may bring your missing car keys. If you are very fortunate, he might bring you a winning lottery ticket.

Pilot stood up and regarded the man who had killed him.

He thought of all the people watching.

He thought of all the animals that Heck Bodkins had killed with the truck.

He thought about how Heck's pride would be hurt.

How he might try again.

Pilot thought hard about what he was going to do next.

Pilot did not maul Heck Bodkins, as he was raised better than that.

Instead, he did a thing that he had once heard of, but had never had a reason to do. He made the greatest roar a bear can make: The White Roar.

The sound and vibration traveled for miles, and was heard and felt within every house and building of Story Town.

Heck Bodkins turned white as a hen's egg and lost all of his hair, save a few tufts here and there. This revealed a tattoo he had concealed for years, which he now regarded as a terribly embarrassing decision from his youth.

He stayed that way for the rest of his life.

He also wet his pants.

To be fair, a lot of people standing nearby also wet their pants.

I did not, however.

At least, not enough that anyone would notice.

Even before he had done it, Pilot had known the effect the White Roar would have on the town that had become his home.

He knew that he would no longer be a man in a bear costume to them.

He would be a real bear. A bear that could hurt or kill. A bear that could roar so loudly that it could tear the hair from a man and forever make him as pale as snow.

Pilot knew he would no longer be welcome in Story Town.

82

There will be times in your life when you become aware that the place you have ended up is wrong for you. That you would be much happier somewhere else.

You may have a job that isn't a good fit, or be with a person who isn't right for you, even if they are wonderful inside.

The moment you become aware of it is a special sort of heartbreak. You will remember how much work it took to get there, and how it felt like home at first. You will think of how hard you've struggled to try and make things work. How you've been told to never give up.

You will realize that when you imagine yourself somewhere very happy, it is a very different place from where you are.

And on that very, very hard day, you will realize you will have to leave.

Leaving can be one of the hardest things you will do in your life.

It might seem like leaving a terrible place is easy, but it is not. When you are in a place that has been wearing you down the whole time you have been there, it makes a happier place seem impossibly far away.

It is tempting to try to think of the days that are not so terrible, to distract yourself.

A terrible situation will devour your strength and courage. Every day it takes away a little of the person you are, and replace it with other little pieces which feel like they don't deserve anything better.

You have to be very brave to leave a place like that.

Leaving a not-terrible place is often harder.

It is an awful feeling to leave a place that is good, but cannot make you happy. To leave a place where there is love, a place that has never tried to hurt you, will tear your heart and make you feel like you are a monster.

The temptation to stay for someone else is so powerful... to be unhappy, but to try and hide it. To behave better and try to forget the life you need, even when you feel as if you are drowning.

You have to be really strong and want what is best for everyone, to leave a place like that.

The bear and the cat left for adventure and to find their places in the world. Sometimes Zipper walked ahead, and sometimes Pilot carried him.

They knew it would be hard at first, but also exciting. It would be an adventure, and adventures often feel that way.

YOU ARE NOW LEAVING STORY TOWN

ORDINARY AMAZING

With Story Town behind them, the cat and the bear both felt very nervous, but also invigorated. As they lumbered on, they felt stronger and braver.

With every step, they walked towards their hopes and their dreams.

With every step, they walked closer to each other.

-

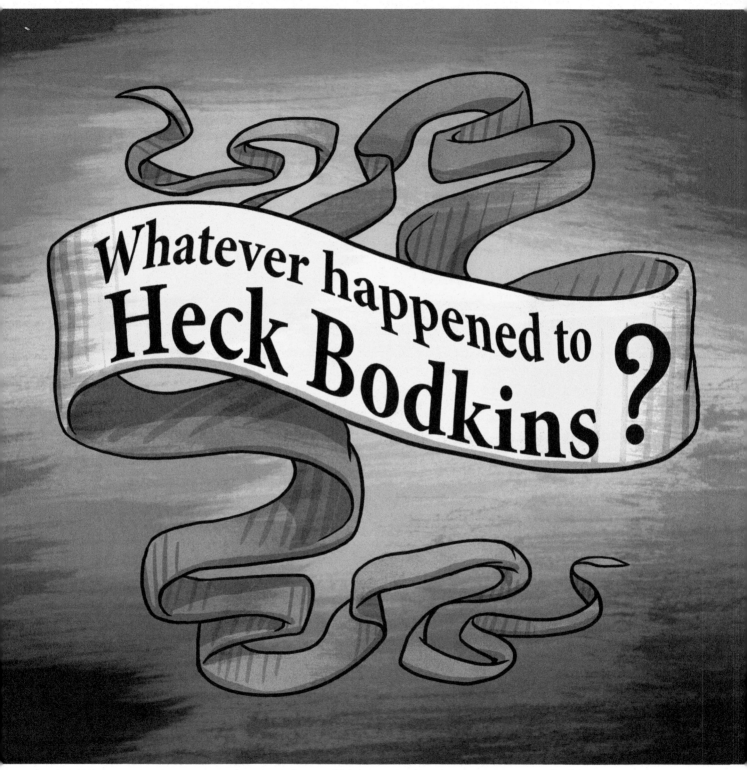

As I mentioned before, the awful Heck Bodkins never showed his face in Story Town ever again.

In fact, now that he was pale and all his hair had fallen out, he never showed his face to anyone at all, if he could help it.

Word had gotten out how it had happened, and how he had run away. The embarassment was too much for him, and burned within him like an angry ember.

If Heck Bodkins had been as mean as a snake before, these days he was meaner than twelve snakes.

MOM

As we know, Heck took his frustrations out on animals. People may have begun to realize how frail and pathetic he was, but a defenseless animal never would.

An animal that was smaller than Heck would always be frightened of him, and that made him feel better. He could kill it easily, and that made him feel even better still. That is just the sort of terrible person he was.

Since the truck had been smashed, Heck stomped through the woods on foot.

94

Jerry the Opossum was looking for berries and acorns to take home to his family. He had hungry little ones at home, and they needed food. They liked berries the best because they were sweet.

Their mother watched them while he scavenged, but they missed their papa.

Jerry would be home soon. He was almost done. They would sleep in a big cozy pile, just as the sun came up.

Once in a while, the littlest of them would wake up and sigh before going back to sleep. Jerry loved that.

97

When Heck Bodkins turned around, the opossum had moved on. He had found enough morsels and was returning home with them.

This made Heck angry, and he walked on to find another creature to be especially cruel to.

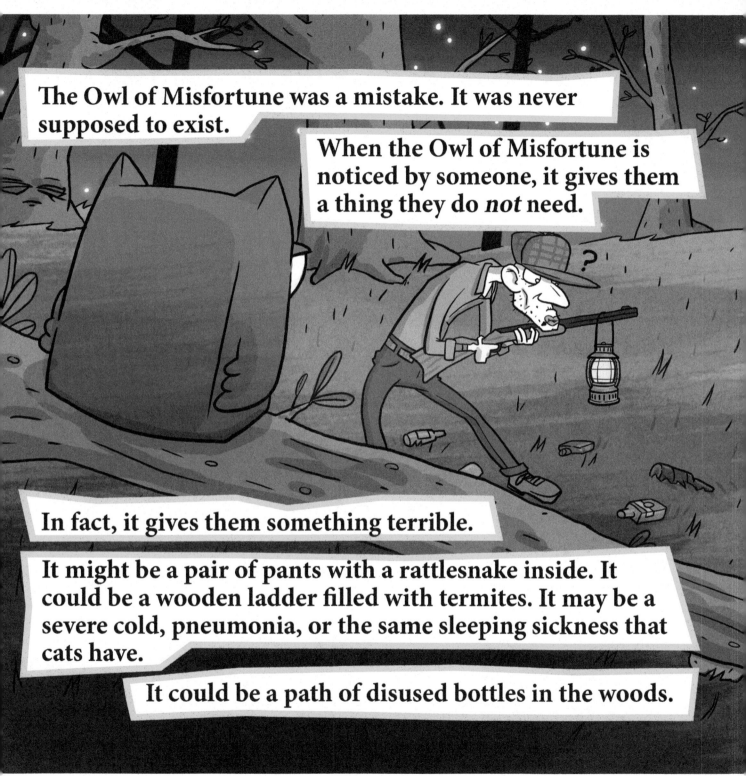

The Owl of Misfortune was a mistake. It was never supposed to exist.

When the Owl of Misfortune is noticed by someone, it gives them a thing they do *not* need.

In fact, it gives them something terrible.

It might be a pair of pants with a rattlesnake inside. It could be a wooden ladder filled with termites. It may be a severe cold, pneumonia, or the same sleeping sickness that cats have.

It could be a path of disused bottles in the woods.

A bear who had grown up with Pilot, but was not as sweet and kind, and was certainly not as forgiving.

A bear who, in fact, became very, very angry when he was disturbed.

In the darkness, Heck Bodkins could not see what happened next. It is to his benefit, and yours, that it was too dark to see.

But he could feel it.

And hear it.

The Owl of Misfortune can see well in the dark, however, and watched the whole thing with interest.

The Owl of Misfortune is a truly horrifing creature, and did not seem to find the visage disturbing in the least.

On the contrary, he seemed quite pleased.

Interactions

Before it is printed into a book, a Story Town adventure is posted online, several pages a day.

At points in the story, readers are asked to make decisions or perform tasks, in order to achieve a certain outcome in the story.

The following pages were seen by readers while "To Lumber Home" was being posted.

Worldsworst's Diner

I did not predict that readers would chose "C" here, but they did. I often will make two reasonable or interesting choices, then one really weird one.

It was close. Bert's Hot Dog Museum had a lot of votes, and it was secretly the one I had *hoped* would be picked. I had some ideas for it already sketched out.

I hadn't really made any plans for Worldsworst, but it was the clear winner. That night, I stayed up and wrote the story of Wallace and how he wanted to have a diner named after him, despite the obvious problems it would cause.

I like Wallace, so as much as I was looking forward to drawing the "World's Oldest Hot Dog," I'm glad it turned out the way it did.

vote for where pilot should work
in this page's comments
at www.story-town.com

Voting will close at 7:00 pm EST

"Chartier's Delight"

Many, many dishes were recommended, and many of them sounded absolutely awful to have to eat. Here are a few notable examples.

Limburger, Liverwurst, and Onions on toast! The "Big Stinky" can be avoided, but never ignored! Optional sauerkraut on the side! - Shaun Brachmann

Spam pate topped with peanut butter mousse on a bed of brussel sprouts puree with chocolate-grapefruit sauce. - Kelly Parker Cobb

Hollowed out log filled with angry hedgehogs and drizzled with bug juices.
- Helen Blaise Lanigan

Haggis, I have no doubt that Pilot could make haggis....but stuffed with gopher sweetbreads, rotten cabbage, and drizzled with honey with a pinch of eu de skunk. - Cricket Chirps

Sour Cream, Lutefisk, and bananas in a beetle butter reduction!
- SinCityFarmGirl
I have a hard time finding good beetle butter. Any ideas? - Me
You can only get it from Beetlebutter's right now. They're working out a deal with Wolrdsworst's, is the scuttlebutt on the street. - SinCityFarmGirl

Toadstool pancakes with foraged mixed wild berries, topped with honey and served with ants on a log (real ants on real sticks) - Karen Chartier

I really liked the idea of actual ants on a log.
Congratulation, Karen!

Dear people.

thank you for all your
nice words. so far
my new job is not
doing good. maybe if
you told me your bad
job storeys i would
feel a little better
adout things. i will write
back. pilot.

I told readers they could write to Pilot.
A lot of people did.
Here are a few of Pilot's responses:

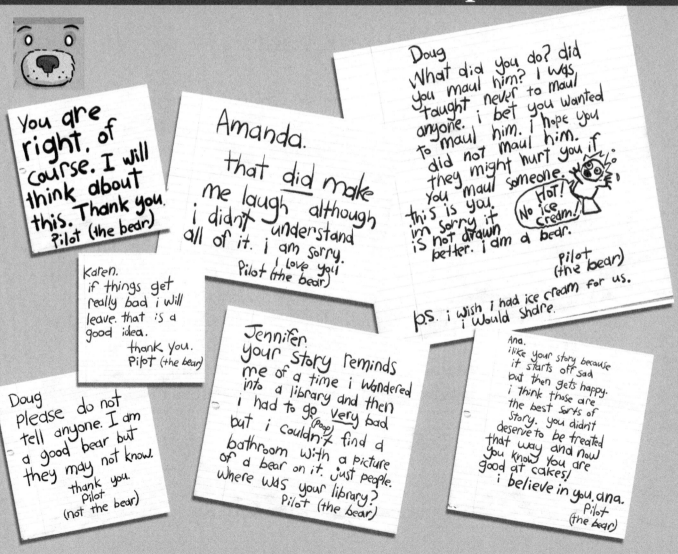

You are right, of course. I will think about this. Thank you.
Pilot (the bear)

Amanda.
that did make me laugh although i didn't understand all of it. i am sorry.
I love you
Pilot (the bear)

Doug
What did you do? did you maul him? I was taught never to maul anyone. i bet you wanted to maul him. i hope you did not maul him. they might hurt you if you maul someone. this is you. im sorry it is not drawn better. i am a bear.
HOT! No ice cream!
Pilot (the bear)
p.s. i wish i had ice cream for us. i would share.

Karen.
if things get really bad i will leave. that is a good idea.
thank you.
Pilot (the bear)

Doug
please do not tell anyone. I am a good bear but they may not know.
thank you.
Pilot (not the bear)

Jennifer.
your story reminds me of a time i wandered into a library and then i had to go very bad (poop) but i couldn't find a bathroom with a picture of a bear on it. just people. where was your library?
Pilot (the bear)

Ana.
i like your story because it starts off sad but then gets happy. i think those are the best sorts of story. you didn't deserve to be treated that way and now you know you are good at cakes! i believe in you. ana.
Pilot (the bear)

I am very grateful to the following people who support the Story Town project through the Red Rocket Farm Patreon page, and by spreading the word of the Story Town series!

THANK YOU!

Dustin Clingman, Allen W. Graham, Laurie, Jennifer Torkkola, Alex Winner, Diana Dobbs, Maria Walters, Michael Ivey, Lela Gouge, Lisette Liang, Anne Robotham, Anne Ferrand, Vicky Salipande, Karen Chartier, Lydia Koenig, Elizabeth Trumbull, Anne Cummings, Mike Weissberg, Kirsten Shelton-Aziz, Doug Gross, Wilson Farrell, Webberly Rattenkraft, Marisol Adams, Catherine Rathbun, Elizabeth Khimani, Steve Blackburn, Jennifer Page Sorenson, James Cook, Amanda Muir, Scott McDaniel, Judith Carney, Regina Melchiorre, Coco Rogers, Heidi Trudell, Alden Levine, Jennifer Barnes, Danielle Hanson, Jennifer Shore, Kendra Sweitzer, Cynthia Choice, Natalie Rosbottom, Helen Blaise Lanigan, Greg Mahler, Kisha Delain, Cricket Chirps, Tabitha Johnston, Adam Hughes everyone else who pledges on Patreon at any level, and Hodgepodge Coffeeshop and Gallery in Atlanta, GA.

www.patreon.com/redrocketfarm

STORY TOWN

BY JASON ALBIN THOMAS

A reader wanted to propose marriage to his girlfriend who was also a Story Town fan. He wanted to give her a ring in a friendship box, so I rushed out these pages to help lead up to the big surprise.

After leaving Story Town, Pilot and Zipper spoke of many things as they walked through the woods.

"Pilot," Zipper asked the bear. "Do you think friendship is like strength? Do you think it is stronger than most things?

"I think it can be," Pilot responded with his deep, but friendly voice. "Whenever two are together they are stronger than one, to be sure."

Pilot continued, "When two are close, especially when there is love... they are stronger than two. They are stronger than one hundred, even."

"Is love stronger than houses?" Zipper asked, his cat eyes wide. Zipper had never known anything stronger than a house before.

"I think two people who love each other can be much stronger than houses. Two people can make each other very strong. They lift each other up.

"A thing that would normally stop or even kill someone... when someone is loved by a good person with all their might... they will slip through as if it were a pile of dry leaves.

"They can do anything. They can do the impossible."

CPSIA information can be obtained
at www.ICGtesting.com
Printed in the USA
LVOW06s0126260416

485257LV00022B/153/P